Dommy B has won many poetry and performance awards, including winning New York's famous Nuyorican Poetry Café Slam, UK's Superheroes of Slam, and *Sabotage Review*'s award for Best Spoken Word Performer. He has been Glastonbury Festival's poet-in-residence and also appeared on BBC's *Rhyme Rocket*.

The Story of the Dragon Who Hates Poetry is adapted from his own poetry theatre show for children and their families.

The *Dragon* series by Dommy B:

The Story of
Spark, the Goblin Wizard

The Story of
When Trolls Try to Eat Your Goldfish

The Story of
The Dragon Who Hates Poetry

The Story of—
Aaaaaaaaaaaaagh! Dinosaurs!

THE STORY OF
THE DRAGON
WHO HATES
POETRY

DOMMY B

Flapjack Press
flapjackpress.co.uk

Exploring the synergy between performance and the page

First published in 2015 by Flapjack Press
Salford, Gtr Manchester
flapjackpress.co.uk

Reprinted in 2018

ISBN 978-0-9576639-7-8

Cover, illustrations & author photo by Brink
paulneads.co.uk

P... P... P... Poems! and Menacing Maze drawn by the author
Dragon Puzzles designed by the author and Brink

Printed by Imprint Digital
Upton Pyne, Exeter, Devon
imprintdigital.com

A version of 'The Dragon Who Hates Poetry' was first published in the
collection *Dommy B vs The Dragon Who Hates Poetry* [Flapjack Press, 2012].

Dedicated to Sergio.
Amazing musician, amazing friend.
True friendship is more powerful than any dragon flame.

CONTENTS

You can watch Dommy B performing 'The Dragon Who Hates Poetry', 'Dragon in My Homework' and 'Dave the Dragon' on YouTube.

CHAPTER ONE

THE DRAGON WHO HATES POETRY

The dragon who hates poetry
is feared throughout the land.
This brutal beast won't back off
until all poetry's banned.

Now every poet's bullied
by his cruel and crazed command.
"FORGET YOUR RHYMING GAME!"
demands the fiend of fire and flame.

There is no dragon scarier,
no, not in any place.

His face looks like his bottom...

...and his bottom like his face.

He'll sneeze out snot as big as rocks.

You'd better clear some space... ... ...*SPLAT!*

"TREMBLE AT MY NAME!"

demands the fiend of fire and flame.

Oh dragon flame! Oh dragon flame!
His face and bum look the same
and he calls every poem lame.
The poets curse the day he came.

Reciting rhymes to roses
was a rhyme lover called Rick.
The dragon sneezed all over him!
It hit Rick like a brick.

A burst of boiling bogeys
left poor Rick feeling quite sick.
"I AM A PERFECT AIM!"
guffawed the fiend of fire and flame.

So poor old Rick stopped reading books.
He said, "Why take the chance?
Instead, I'll stitch my verse into
spare pairs of underpants."

The dragon saw his washing line.
Without a second glance,

"YOUR WORDS I'LL MAUL AND MAIM!"

he roared. Rick's pants went up in flame.

Then Suzie Sue the farmer
felt so very sad and blue.
She whispered verse in horses' ears.
A harmless thing to do.

When dragon bawled, she fainted,
fell face-first in... pony poo.
"JUST GOT YOURSELF TO BLAME!"
called out the fiend of fire and flame.

Oh dragon flame! Oh dragon flame
leaves poets feeling fear and shame.
Is there nobody who can tame
this flagrant fiend of fire and flame?

CHAPTER TWO
RICK AND THE DRAGON

There is an urgent village meeting about how to stop the dragon.

Rhyming Rick desperately wants to go to the meeting, but the dragon has burned all the clothes on his washing line.

Now Rick doesn't have any underpants to wear.

In fact, all Rick has to wear to the meeting is...

...an empty old barrel.

As Rick walks from his house to the meeting (in his barrel) a dark, menacing shadow falls over the land.

Something big is flying up above Rick's head.

The dragon!

"Arrrrrrrrgh! Mr Dragon! Please don't eat me!"

"WHAT DO YOU THINK YOU ARE DOING, YOU HORRIBLE, YOU HIDEOUS, YOU... *DELICIOUS* LOOKING LITTLE HUMAN? ARE YOU THINKING OF WRITING ANY... P... P... P... P... POEMS?"

"No! No! No!" Rick shivers.

"I'm not doing any harm! Just walking down the *street*. Please, oh dragon, let me go. I'll beat a quick *retreat*."

"STREET, BEAT... AND RETREAT... THOSE ARE *RHYMING* WORDS!"

"No! No! No!" howls Rick. "What I meant to say was... I don't want to upset you. I think you're really *sweet!* I'm too tired to try to rhyme, exhausted head to... *feet*."

"STREET? BEAT? RETREAT, SWEET, FEET? THIS SOUNDS TO ME LIKE... LIKE... LIKE... A P... P... POEM!"

The dragon roars and spits a giant sheet of golden flames into the air!

"No! No! No!" wails Rick.

"Please be kind and don't *mistreat me.*
I'll go now. I'll go *discreetly.*
I'll go calmly. I'll go *neatly.*
Please just promise you won't... ...*eat me.*"

The dragon opens his enormous mouth. His breath smells like barbecued socks.

Rick runs, and the dragon gives chase.

Rick runs through the streets, past the school, past the shops... imagine how hard it is to run wearing a barrel!

There it is – the meeting is in the house right ahead! Rick dives out the way of a bolt of flame and slams the house door shut behind him.

Outside, the dragon roars.

"YOU HORRIBLE LITTLE HUMAN! NO MORE... P... P... P... POEMS... OR I'LL BURN YOU ALIVE!"

With that, the dragon flies away.

CHAPTER THREE

DRAGONS ARE FANTASTIC

From the crowd inside the house, Suzie Sue the farmer steps forward.

"That dragon must be so sad," says Suzie Sue. "He can't even say the word 'poem' without being sick. We should write a poem about dragons! If the dragon read a poem all about him, I'm sure he would love it."

Rick isn't sure. "I don't want the dragon to... eat me!"

"But you're the best rhymer in the village, Rick," say all the other villagers. "You've got to do it. Please!"

Rick works all afternoon writing his dragon poem.

Dragons are fantastic!
Dragons are great!
I would love a dragon
as my mate!

Dragons love collecting gold.
They're bold and brave and strong.
Talked about in poetry
and sung about in song.

Breathing flames, they never
need a lighter or a match.
Dragon mums are proud
to watch their dragon eggs all hatch.

Baby dragons look so cute.
Their wisdom runs so deep.
Always keeping one eye open
- even when asleep.

Dragons are fantastic!
Dragons are great!
I would love a dragon
as my mate!

"Hold on!" says Suzie Sue. "We can't write this poem on a piece of paper."

"Why?" asks Rick.

"It will be too small. Dragons fly high in the sky. They look down from above. We need something greater than a little piece of paper."

"Like what?" ask the villagers.

"I know!" Suzie Sue clicks her fingers. "Let's get this poem up in the trees! Let's make a poem out of... the forest!"

The villagers work together for three days to get the poem into the woods.

They pull tree branches together and tie them with thick ropes to make giant letters.

The villagers get Rick tough, new work clothes so that he can climb up and help.

(He couldn't really climb up there wearing a barrel.)

By the third day the poem is finished.

"What a beautiful poem it is," remarks Rick.

"Look!" Suzie Sue points to the sky. "The dragon is coming!"

The dragon hovers in mid-air. He reads every word of the poem in the trees. Then...

...he blows out a huge fireball!

"NO MORE WARNINGS. YOU ARE ALL GOING TO BURN! IF ANY OF YOU TRY TO ESCAPE, I WILL FIND YOU... AND I WILL EAT YOU!"

CHAPTER FOUR

WHY THE DRAGON HATES POETRY

The dragon flies away. All around fire flickers!

"Water!" screams Suzie Sue. "Bring buckets of water. Throw the water over the trees."

They put out the fire... but a lot of trees are badly burnt.

The poem is destroyed.

Rick feels more angry than he has ever felt before.

"Why does the dragon hate poetry?" he shouts. "I love poetry. Poetry is exciting, funny and imaginative. How dare the dragon set fire to my poem! I'm going to go to his home and I'm going to make him stop."

"No, Rick, no!" plead the villagers. "He'll eat you up! The best idea is to stop writing. Then we'll be safe."

"Stop writing? I'll never stop writing. I'm not scared of a dragon who hates poetry. I am a poet!"

Rick strides out of the village and marches all the way through the burnt forest.

On the other side is a tall, craggy mountain. Full of rage, Rick climbs up to the top. There he finds...

...the dragon, curled up like a giant snake in his cave.

"WHO DARES DISTURB ME? OH. IT'S YOU. PESKY HUMAN. GO AWAY OR I'LL CRUSH YOUR BONES!"

Rick is really frightened, but doesn't let it show.

"No! I won't leave until you tell me why you hate poems."

"NO DRAGONS LIKE... POEMS. ONLY SILLY PEOPLE LIKE... POEMS!"

"Well, only silly dragons burn poems. Have you ever had something you've made be destroyed by somebody else? Have you ever written a poem?"

"WHAT? NO! IF I TRIED TO WRITE A... POEM YOU'D TELL ME I'D GOT IT WRONG. YOU'D CALL ME STUPID."

"Stupid? No. I won't call you stupid. I promise. What's your name, dragon?"

"MY NAME? NOBODY HAS EVER ASKED FOR MY NAME BEFORE. IT'S BEEN SO LONG, I CAN BARELY REMEMBER IT MYSELF.

IS IT... *MAZE?*

IS IT... *GARLIC MAYONNAISE?*

IS IT... *SPAGHETTI BOLOGNAISE?*

NO, NO, NO, NO, NO...

IS IT... IS IT... *BLAZE?*

YES!
BLAZE THE DRAGON.
THAT'S MY NAME!
BLAZE!"

"Blaze the dragon," Rick repeats. "I like that name. Blaze is such a fiery name, on that we all agree... That could be the first line of a poem. What's another word that means 'fiery'?"

"WHAT? I DON'T KNOW. I'M TOO TOUGH FOR ALL THIS."

"Tough! Brilliant! Toughest dragon in the village, anyone can see. Powerful... and..."

"POWERFUL... AND MUSCULAR."

"Powerful and muscular, now you listen to..."

"TO... ... ...TO ME?"

"Yes! Blaze the dragon is so strong... and he loves poetry!

Blaze is such a fiery name,
on that we all agree.
Toughest dragon in the village,
anyone can see.
Powerful and muscular,
now you listen to me.
Blaze the dragon is so strong...
and he loves poetry!"

Blaze starts to blush.

Have you ever seen a dragon blush? It is redder than any human.

"THIS IS THE FIRST TIME ANYONE'S EVER COME UP HERE TO MY CAVE. IT'S THE FIRST TIME ANYONE'S TOLD ME A... POEM.

NO ONE'S EVER REALLY SPOKEN TO ME BEFORE TODAY.

**WAIT A MINUTE, WAIT A MINUTE...
PO... ... ...EM!
POEM!
THAT'S THE FIRST TIME I'VE EVER
SAID THAT WORD WITHOUT FEELING
SICK. IN FACT, IT'S A LOVELY WORD!
POEM!"**

Rick and Blaze become the best of friends.

They write many more poems together and even win competitions with their words.

They win the first annual Village Verse Poetry Slam, hosted by Suzie Sue (whose pony poo poem gets a big laugh).

People in the village stop being afraid of Blaze and start to cheer the pair on whenever they perform.

Rhyming Rick and Blaze the dragon become the biggest poetry double act the forest has ever seen.

P... P... P... POEMS!

Here are two of the many poems Blaze and Rick have written together. Rick has even drawn some pictures to go with them.

Both poems are about other dragons, dragons that are very different to each other. The dragon in the second poem is a really friendly dragon. The dragon in the first poem... is not.

I walk to school. I hear a crack.
A dragon bursts from the tarmac!
Its nasty claws taut for attack.
Its lips are wet. Its jaw is slack.

No beast will eat me for a snack!
I have no muscles (no six-pack),
but I've the brains that dragons lack.
I trap it in my maths book!

Although I know I'm no hero
I *did* just catch a dragon... so...
I raise my book and cheer "BRAVO!"
Should I hand in my homework...?

A dragon's trapped between these pages.
Must keep this book shut for ages.

"Sir!" I yell, "Don't look below
my maths book's cover!" (Now aglow,
as from inside dark smoke rings blow!)
Should I hand in my homework...?

"Without a sword, without crossbow,
without kung-fu or tae-kwon-do,
with just my book I caught this foe."
Should I hand in my homework...?

My teacher says, "What nonsense. Right,
You gave the whole class quite a fright."
He takes the book. Its spine glows bright.
Its pages smoulder fiery light.

"No...!" I yell. "Look, I'll rewrite
my homework, please, I'll do it tonight!"
He opens the book... The dragon takes flight...
and gobbles him up in one sharp bite!

Teachers! My moral is more than implied.
I'd hate to corrupt. Don't mean to misguide.
When you mark homework keep caution applied...
There might be a dragon...

waiting...

inside!

DAVE THE DRAGON

I have a pet dragon called Dave.
His mouth is as dark as a cave.
His wings are bright red,
he's as big as a shed
and sometimes he does... misbehave.

Oh, Dave is not nasty or cruel,
but once, he flew over my school.
He needed a drink
and before I could blink
he drunk up the school swimming pool!

The teacher said, "Ooh, this looks grim.
Now where can we go for a swim?"
I had an idea,
put my mouth to Dave's ear
and this is what I said to him:

"We can save the day - you and me.
Let's fly, on your back, to the sea!"
Dave flew us outside,
a trip to the seaside,
and everyone shouted "Yippee!"

DRAGON PUZZLES

Rick has started writing a new poem, which he now wants to finish writing with Blaze.

However, to reach Blaze, Rick must get through a deadly maze full of other dragons... dragons who all hate poems, but love eating poets!

Can you guide Rick from **START** all the way to the arrow leading out of the maze?

If you run into a dragon's big, sharp teeth it will eat you! Game over!

You can pass a dragon safely if you are moving towards its wings and tail. Then you can jump over its back and carry on forwards without getting swallowed whole!

Don't get stuck!

Can you find all of the words hidden in this puzzle?
They go up, down, diagonally and back to front!

B	K	S	E	T	M	U	W	F
D	O	C	A	Y	I	F	E	I
W	A	T	I	X	D	A	G	P
F	G	M	T	R	X	R	P	O
L	X	R	U	O	B	M	K	E
U	D	E	Q	L	M	E	J	M
N	M	U	A	O	S	R	W	C
W	H	Z	E	M	Y	H	R	P
O	E	V	I	L	L	A	G	E

BLAZE   FACE

RHYME   BOTTOM

RICK   VILLAGE

POEM   FARMER

Across:

2. Blaze's breath smells like barbecued _ _ _ _ _ (5)
4. Yuck! It's pony _ _ _ (3)
5. Blaze sneezes this, as big as rocks (4)
7. Rick had to wear one (6)
10. Rick sewed poems into... what? (10)
11. Blaze is such a _ _ _ _ _ name (5)

Down:

1. Blaze couldn't say this without feeling sick (6)
2. She's the village farmer (5,3)
3. Outside Blaze's cave were warning... what? (5)
6. The villagers built a poem out of these (5)
8. Blaze is a fiend of fire and _ _ _ _ _ (5)
9. Blaze's face looks like his... what? (3)

Blaze finished writing a new poem with Rick... but then he sneezed all over it.

The brand new poem is now caked in snot!

Rick is desperate to remember what the words were which are now all covered in bogeys.

"Blaze, we will never win this year's Village Verse Poetry Slam if we don't complete this poem," warns Rick.

Can you help Blaze and Rick work out the last word in each rhyme?

Women worried,
Men were manic.
Blaze made
everybody _____.
Roaring, clawing,
soaring higher,
breathing smoking
sheets of _____.
Don't get scared
or in a state,
this fire-breather
is our _____.

There are six differences between these two pictures.

Can you spot all of them?

Can you find these hidden words?
They go up, down, diagonally and back to front!

F	N	I	A	T	N	U	O	M	B	G
A	L	D	R	A	Q	X	N	R	E	N
N	A	L	K	A	F	P	I	L	O	I
T	N	U	A	M	O	L	B	I	S	Z
A	W	F	O	B	L	M	Q	W	I	A
S	B	Z	O	I	E	F	Y	L	R	M
T	E	O	A	R	G	R	C	G	U	A
I	D	N	T	U	E	Y	I	E	Q	F
C	T	I	Q	N	Z	S	B	F	F	U
L	G	R	E	A	T	X	T	T	F	I
N	O	G	A	R	D	S	M	O	K	E

DRAGON	TREMBLE
FANTASTIC	FIREBALL
AMAZING	SMOKE
BRILLIANT	FOREST
GREAT	MOUNTAIN

Crafty Crossword

Across: 2. SOCKS, 4. POO, 5. SNOT, 7. BARREL, 10. UNDERPANTS, 11. FIERY
Down: 1. POETRY, 2. SUZIE SUE, 3. SIGNS, 6. TREES, 8. FLAME, 9. BUM

Wicked Wordsearch One

Wicked Wordsearch Two

F	N	I	A	T	N	U	O	M	B	G
A	L	D	R	A	Q	X	N	R	E	N
N	A	L	K	A	F	P	I	L	O	I
T	N	U	A	M	O	L	B	I	S	Z
A	W	F	O	B	L	M	Q	W	I	A
S	B	Z	O	I	E	F	Y	L	R	M
T	E	O	A	R	G	R	C	G	U	A
I	D	N	T	U	E	Y	I	E	Q	F
C	T	I	Q	N	Z	S	B	F	F	U
L	G	R	E	A	T	X	T	T	F	I
N	O	G	A	R	D	S	M	O	K	E

Dangerous Differences

Ridiculous Rhymes

PANIC, FIRE, MATE